## Historical Setting

In December 2019, a deadly coronavirus was found in China. The main symptoms of the illness were a high temperature, a new and continuous cough, and a loss of, or change to, a person's sense of taste or smell. The infection quickly spread worldwide.

To stop the spread of this disease, people with COVID-19 symptoms were asked to self-isolate and stay at home with their families for a set number of days. Everyone was told to keep two metres away from people they did not live with. Sometimes a lockdown was enforced, which meant that everybody had to stay at home, and they did not have freedom to do their normal activities.

Eventually, coronavirus tests became available. At this point, people did not have to self-isolate if the test showed that they were free from the disease. Coronavirus vaccines were developed to help society get back to normality. During 2021, many people around the world had the vaccines. Unlike in this story, the vaccines were not plant based.

SG - For my sons and the many children who showed courage during the COVID-19 pandemic.

First published in Great Britain in 2022 by:
Faithful Stories Limited
www.faithfulstories.com

Text copyright © Stacey Gittens 2022
Illustrations copyright © Gail Yerrill 2022

Stacey Gittens and Gail Yerrill have asserted their right to be identified
as the Author and Illustrator of this work in accordance with the
Copyright, Designs and Patents Act 1988.

A CIP catalogue record for this book is available from the British Library.
Paperback ISBN 978-1-7397735-0-2

Design & Layout by: Happydesigner
www.happydesigner.co.uk

# This book belongs to:

1 .......Daniel Dinosaur.......

2 ..........................................

3 ..........................................

4 ..........................................

5 ..........................................

6 ..........................................

7 ..........................................

*Sharing stories with the generations that follow.*

ROAR

# Daniel Dinosaur's Dilemmas

## Stacey Gittens

Illustrations by Gail Yerrill

*Can you imagine what it would be like if dinosaurs lived today?*
*And how, if one was your classmate, he'd scare the teachers away?*
*This is the tale of Daniel, and one very strange school year,*
*And all the emotions this T. rex felt as he overcame his fear.*

Daniel Dinosaur lived in a large village in England called Wootton. This place was nestled within the Forest of Marston Vale, where Daniel freely roamed.

Daniel was a kind and friendly dinosaur, but when he smiled, children were **AFRAID** of his pointy, white, shiny teeth, and they would run away.

Daniel would call out to them, but his loud **ROAR** echoed for miles, and everyone who heard it trembled.

ROAR

This made Daniel **SAD** because he wanted to have friends.

When Daniel was old enough to go to school, he was so **EXCITED**.

He could not wait to learn and play with his classmates.

However, on his way to school, Daniel began to WORRY.

What if he scared everyone away with his smile and roar?

Daniel quickly decided that he would always keep his mouth shut at school.

As Daniel hurried through the school gate, he held his breath and shut his mouth tightly. When he reached his classroom door, his new teacher smiled at him.

Welcome.
I am so **GLAD**
you are here.

As Daniel waved to her in reply, his excitement overwhelmed him and he felt his roar bubbling up inside.

The roar tickled his throat so much that he began to cough quite loudly, and his lack of breath made the coughing worse.

The teacher said to Daniel...

You must go
home and take a test.
If you don't pass it,
you must stay at
home for ten days.
**DO NOT SEE
ANYONE!**

Daniel was CONFUSED.
He had not learnt anything
at school.

There is no way
I can pass a test.
I'll come back to
school in ten days.

Ten days later, Daniel was still ANXIOUS
that people would think he was a scary dinosaur.

As Daniel scampered towards the school gate, he wanted to
reassure everyone that he did not want to hunt or eat people.
So Daniel shouted...

"I can't smell anything!
I can't taste anything!"

As soon as Daniel spoke, the teacher at the gate said...

You must go home and take a test. If you don't pass it, you must stay at home for ten days. **DO NOT SEE ANYONE!**

Daniel was PERPLEXED as he still had not learnt anything at school.

There is no way I can pass a test. I'll come back to school in ten days.

During the 20 days he was cooped up at home, Daniel did not notice the weather turning colder. So he did not wear his coat when he went back to school.

When Daniel entered the playground, he started to shiver terribly.

Daniel did not want to be sent home for being too COLD, so he started to sing...

Immediately, a passing teacher asked,
"Do you know what your temperature is?"
Daniel wanted to seem smart. "Yes, I do!"
"Do you know how many degrees?"
Daniel thought she asked, "How many trees?"

Daniel could see lots of trees. He silently calculated,
*Mum is 41 years old and that's a big number!*
"41," he declared, hoping this was enough.
"41!" exclaimed the teacher...

You must go
home and take a test.
If you don't pass it,
you must stay at
home for ten days.
**DO NOT SEE
ANYONE!**

Daniel was
**BEWILDERED**
as he still had not learnt
anything at school.

There is no way
I can pass a test.
I'll come back to
school in ten days.

Ten more **LONELY** days passed. More than ever, Daniel longed to make friends.

**I AM SOOOO LONELY!**

When the day came for Daniel to return to school, he gargled with salt to settle his roars. He put on his coat to ensure he was just the right temperature. He packed a huge lunchbox so everyone would know that he did not want to eat humans.

Daniel started to feel NERVOUS as he walked to school because the streets were silent and deserted. Mr Tavener, the head teacher, stood alone outside the school.

Mr Tavener spoke kindly. "Children can come to school if their parents have jobs that help others. Most students must stay at home and do **ONLINE** learning. This will keep families safe from the virus, which has made a lot of people very sick. Things can go back to normal when a special medicine for this disease is discovered."

Daniel was **UPSET** because he did not know when he would return to school. He scurried home with tears in his eyes.

As the weeks passed,
Daniel felt **FRUSTRATED**.

He was determined to learn,
but he did not know how to
do it **ONLINE**.

Daniel knew that he, like all T. rex dinosaurs, had much
better vision than any human, so he looked for
**ONLINE** opportunities.

As Daniel crept into the surrounding forest, he prayed for
answers and guidance. Daniel believed that if he had faith,
miracles were possible.

In the distance, Daniel spotted a **LINE** of bushes, which held hundreds of delicate purple wildflowers with specks of gold in their centres.

For the first time in his life, Daniel embraced his dinosaur traits. At a speed of eight metres per second, he rushed to stomp **ON** the **LINE** of flowers.

His extra-strong feet crushed the **LINE** of bushes,
revealing millions of tasty seeds.

Daniel carefully carried lots of the seeds home to show Daisy, his mum.

Mum, I found these unusual seeds while doing some **ONLINE** learning. Do you think they could be used in the special medicine for the virus?

That's a great idea, Daniel! I will take these seeds to my friend, Tee. She works with medicines, and she will be able to investigate them.

Daniel was extremely **HAPPY**.

Months passed. Daniel was losing hope. Then one day, the phone rang. As Daisy listened to the caller, her face lit up.

She was **SURPRISED**.

"Daniel, you did it!" she exclaimed. "Your plant is the perfect medicine to protect people from the virus. You can now go back to school. **HOORAY!**"

Overflowing with **JOY**, Daniel hugged Daisy.

Daniel's prayers had been answered, and he felt so **GRATEFUL**.

Not long after, on a warm spring day, Daniel danced all the way to school. Finally, he felt **CONFIDENT** that he would make new friends.

Daniel approached his teacher. Before she had the chance to speak, Daniel handed her this note:

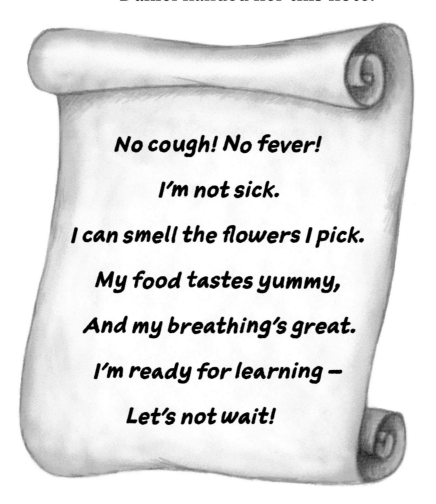

No cough! No fever!

I'm not sick.

I can smell the flowers I pick.

My food tastes yummy,

And my breathing's great.

I'm ready for learning –

Let's not wait!

Daniel's teacher beamed.

Welcome.
I am **THRILLED** to
be teaching a famous
superhero.

At long last, Daniel was PROUD of his dinosaur qualities,
and he was **DELIGHTED** to be different.

In the summer, it was Daniel's birthday.
All his new friends came for **SOFT PLAY**.
He never again tried to hide his roar,
And everyone loved Daniel Dinosaur!

# Tips for Readers and Grown-Ups

**Reading the Book**

Younger readers can develop their literacy skills by listening to the story as well as by sounding out and reading aloud the emphasised words within the text.

More confident readers can either listen to the story for pleasure or can read the text aloud to a grown-up. The meaning of some new words can be decoded by identifying synonyms (words that have the same meaning) in the story.

**Synonym examples:**

1) Confused, perplexed and bewildered.

2) Hurried, scurried and rushed.

**Asking Questions**

Making inferences is also an important skill to develop. Grown-ups can help readers to do this by asking them questions such as:

1) Does Daniel want to go to school? How do you know this?

2) What does Daniel fear the most? Which words in the story give you that impression?

3) Why does Daniel pray for help?

4) Can you explain why Daisy was surprised? What makes you think that?

5) Can you choose an interesting word in the book and tell me what you think it means?

6) Why is Daniel confident towards the end of the story?

**Discussion Topics**

The text contains vocabulary that will help readers share their own feelings and personal experiences. Likewise, the character illustrations are visual prompts that can help teach children how to recognise other people's feelings.

This book demonstrates the importance of embracing different physical traits and emotional responses. More established readers may wish to explore the following questions:

1) What qualities and traits make me unique? Am I proud of these qualities or do I try and hide these from others?

2) Should people try to hide their differences? Why or why not?

3) How can we help other people to feel good about themselves?

HAPPY
DELIGHTED
THRILLED

SAD
UPSET
LONELY

WORRIED
ANXIOUS
NERVOUS

CONFUSED
PERPLEXED
BEWILDERED

GRATEFUL
THANKFUL

AFRAID
SCARED

FRUSTRATED
ANGRY

SICK
POORLY

CONFIDENT

EXCITED

PROUD

SURPRISED

# 'Thank You' to our Sponsors

Your positivity and willingness to bring joy
to others has been inspirational.

www.gailyerrill.co.uk

www.happydesigner.co.uk

www.concordeblinds.com

www.127consultancies.com

www.woottonrangers.com

www.belmontguard.co.uk

www.wavendonautosales.com

www.theconversionguys.co.uk

## A Message from the Author

The global impact of the COVID-19 pandemic created challenges and hardships for many people. As a family, we looked for the positives during lockdowns and we found joy in new hobbies, such as gardening and painting rainbow pictures for our windows, as did so many other families.

During this time, I found strength and comfort in this Bible proverb:

> *'Trust in the LORD with all your heart,*
> *And lean not on your own understanding.*
> *In all your ways acknowledge Him,*
> *And He shall direct your paths.'*
> *Proverbs 3:5–6 (New King James Version)*

I wrote this book to encourage other people to remain positive in times of trials. As a way to further help others, I have decided to donate some of the proceeds from the sale of this book to various charities and not-for-profit organisations. This is possible because sponsors and volunteers have donated their time, skills and resources to produce this keepsake. Words alone cannot express my appreciation.

In this story, Daniel explores, learns, discovers and prays within the Forest of Marston Vale. I wish to acknowledge the importance of preserving our forests and protecting the flora and wildlife that live within these sanctuaries. A big thank you is due to all readers who treat our forests with care and respect when visiting.